Prairie Primer

A to Z

by Caroline Stutson

illustrated by Susan Condie Lamb

PUFFIN BOOKS

PUFFIN BOOKS
Published by the Penguin Group
Penguin Putnam Books for Young Readers, 345 Hudson Street, New York, New York 10014, U.S.A.
Penguin Books Ltd, 27 Wrights Lane, London W8 5TZ, England
Penguin Books Australia Ltd, Ringwood, Victoria, Australia
Penguin Books Canada Ltd, 10 Alcorn Avenue, Toronto, Ontario, Canada M4V 3B2
Penguin Books (N.Z.) Ltd, 182-190 Wairau Road, Auckland 10, New Zealand

Penguin Books Ltd, Registered Offices: Harmondsworth, Middlesex, England

First published in the United States of America by Dutton Children's Books, a division of Penguin Books USA Inc., 1996
Published by Puffin Books, a member of Penguin Putnam Books for Young Readers, 1999

10 9 8 7 6 5 4 3 2 1

Text copyright © Caroline Stutson, 1996
Illustrations copyright © Susan Condie Lamb, 1996
All rights reserved

THE LIBRARY OF CONGRESS HAS CATALOGED THE DUTTON EDITION AS FOLLOWS:
Stutson,Caroline.
Prairie Primer / by Caroline Stutson; illustrated by Susan Condie Lamb.—1st ed.   p.   cm.
Summary: Life on the prairie is depicted in this rhyming alphabet book.
ISBN 0-525-45163-3 (hc.)
[1. Frontier and pioneer life—Fiction. 2. Stories in rhyme. 3. Alphabet.] I. Lamb, Susan Condie, ill. II. Title.
PZ8.3.S925Pr 1996 [E]—dc20 95-45811 CIP AC

Puffin Books ISBN 0-14-056551-5

Printed in the United States of America

To Candace, with love
With special thanks to the Littleton Historical Museum

C.S.

To Chris, Charlie, and Ella—
for believing that painted pies are just as yummy

S.C.L.

A the Alphabet I'll learn

B for Butter in the churn

C so Cozy by the stove

D we're rolling out the Dough

E brown Eggs I mustn't drop

F the Firewood we chop

G for greedy Guinea hens

H the House that calls us in

"Coming! Coming!" we all sing,
on the porch for one last swing.

I two Irons growing hot,
breakfast porridge in the pot

When the bowls are
cleared away...

J a game of Jacks we play.

Long black stockings,
high-top shoes,

K
for Knickers and
Kazoos

L the Lunch pails packed for school

M this trifling, stubborn Mule!

 **N** for one bad Nanny goat,
pulling buttons from my coat

O our Oxen in the pen

P there's Piggy out again!

Sunday morning, dressed for church,
down the road we bump and lurch.

 **Q** for Quiet much too long

R the rafters Ring with song!

Fabric scraps of green and purple,

S

for ladies' Sewing circle

T

Teetotum spins for fun

U

Umbrella shades the sun

Pedals flying, racing speed,

V

a blue Velocipede!

Carved by Papa...
bright and big,

W

new Whirligig

Count the crosses Sister's stitched...
her first sampler made with **X**

Y another Year for me
with birthday cake beneath the tree

Z the days Zipped by so fast
but now it's time for bed at last...
now it's time for bed at last.